STELLA ★ THE STAR

MARK SHULMAN

Illustrations by
VINCENT NGUYEN

WALKER & COMPANY ✸ NEW YORK

For Barbara and Bill, the parents I learn from most —M. S.
To Peter Nguyen and Katherine Nix for their support —V. N.

First published in the United States of America in 2004 by
Walker Publishing Company, Inc.

Published simultaneously in Canada by Fitzhenry and Whiteside, Markham, Ontario L3R 4T8

For information about permission to reproduce selections from this book,
write to Permissions, Walker & Company, 104 Fifth Avenue, New York, New York 10011

Library of Congress Cataloging-in-Publication Data

Shulman, Mark, 1962-
Stella the star / Mark Shulman ; illustrations by Vincent Nguyen.
p. cm.
Summary: Stella's parents are very proud when they learn that she will be the "star" in her school play.
ISBN 0-8027-8894-7 (hc) — ISBN 0-8027-8895-5 (re)
[1. Theater—Fiction. 2. Schools—Fiction. 3. Parent and child—Fiction.] I. Nguyen, Vincent, ill. II. Title.

PZ7.S559445St 2004
[E]—dc22
2003057157

The artist used oil paints on prepared paper to create the illustrations for this book.
The author saw a quick sketch of Stella and her costume in the artist's sketchbook
and wrote this story for her.

Book design by Nicole Gastonguay

Visit Walker & Company's Web site at www.walkeryoungreaders.com

Printed in Hong Kong

2 4 6 8 10 9 7 5 3 1

Stella came home from school with a note from Miss Jodi.

"What's it say, Mama?"

Mama opened the note. "The school is putting on a play," she said. Then her eyes opened wide. "My goodness, Stella, Miss Jodi wants *you* to be the star!"

"The star," repeated Stella. "Is that good, Mama?"

"It's like being the queen," said Mama. "That makes me so proud."

Stella looked up. "I want you to be proud, Mama."

That evening, Papa burst through the door holding a shiny
pink-and-silver bag.

"Hello, my little star!" said Papa, in his big overcoat.

Stella jumped up and hugged her papa as far around as her
arms would go. "But it's not my birthday, Papa. And it's not
Christmas. How come I get my special candy?"

"Because you're the star," said Papa, laughing. "I'm very
proud of you."

Stella nodded. "I want you to be proud, Papa."

Mama said there wasn't much time to get Stella ready for her play. A star like Stella needed new things. Mama had a list.

At the shoe store, Mama told the clerk all about Stella's play. "More than twenty-three children will be on that stage. But my Stella's the star."

"That's very nice," said the clerk. "Shall I wrap these?"

At the dress store, Mama and Papa said no to a hundred dresses before they found one that was good enough. "Because," said Papa, "Stella will be meeting so many people after the play." "How lovely," said the busy owner.

The hair salon was not the kind that takes little girls, but Mama insisted. Stella could not sit still. "You never know," said Mama. "I've seen famous children in movies. And our Stella has *so* much talent."

"So I see," said the tired hairdresser.

Stella was tired too, and hungry, and she wanted to go home. But Papa said they had one more stop.

"A video camera, please. I can't miss a moment of my Stella's play."

The salesman knew all about proud papas. "We have good, better, and best cameras," he said.

"Oh, I need the very, very best for our star," announced Papa.

The salesman smiled. "Of course."

Stella slept all the way home.

At school, on the afternoon of the play, Stella began to get excited. "Now remember," said Mama, brushing Stella's hair, "after the play we're taking you to a very fancy restaurant."

"But Mama, after the play all the kids are having ice cream in the basement. Can't I have ice cream too?"

"Oh no," said Mama. "Ice cream in the basement is not good enough for the star. Only the best restaurant. We want to show everyone how proud we are!"

"I want you to be proud," said Stella, quietly.

Miss Jodi appeared in the crowded hall and took Stella's hand. "Time for our little star to get into her costume," she announced. Mama and Papa just stood there, glowing with pride.

Mama and Papa needed half the seats in the front row.

They had their snapshot camera. They had their video
camera. They had a big red bouquet of roses for Stella. They
told all the other parents their Stella was the star.

The play finally began. Mama and Papa
waited very eagerly to see Stella take the stage.

And waited.

And waited.

The play was almost over. Where was Stella? Mama
and Papa grew worried. Was something wrong? And then . . .

Onto the stage marched Stella, dressed like a star—
a star in the sky, next to a boy dressed like the moon.

"Twinkle, twinkle," said Stella, perfectly. Then she smiled
a brilliant smile, waved to her parents, and marched right off
the stage again.

When she found her parents in the hall, Stella was thrilled. "Did you see me in the play? Did you see me? I was the star!"

"Yes you were," said Papa, with a very quiet laugh. "You were a wonderful star."

Mama tried to keep chocolate ice cream off Stella's new dress, but it was too late. All the kids in the basement were messy.

"You made us very proud today, Stella," said Mama, and she meant it.

"Good," said Stella, licking her fingers. "That's just what I wanted."